Incy Wincy Spider

For Ben and James

A Lothian Children's Book
Published in Australia and New Zealand in 2014
by Hachette Australia
Level 17, 207 Kent Street, Sydney NSW 2000
www.hachettechildrens.com.au

10 9 8 7 6 5 4 3 2 1

National Library of Australia
Cataloguing-in-Publication data:

Erasmus, Karen.
Incy Wincy Spider / illustrated by Karen Erasmus.

978 0 7344 1548 6 (hbk.)
978 0 7344 1549 3 (pbk.)

A823.4

Designed by Ingrid Kwong
Colour reproduction by Splitting Image
Printed in China by Toppan Leefung

Incy Wincy Spider

Illustrated by
Karen Erasmus

LOTHIAN Children's Books

The Incy Wincy Spider climbed up the waterspout.

Down came the rain
and **Washed** poor Incy out.

The Incy Wincy Spider
climbed up the verandah steps.

Over walked Grandpa
and **out** poor Incy was **swept.**

The Incy Wincy Spider climbed under the house.

Around came the cat

and thought Incy was a mouse!

The Incy Wincy Spider
climbed up the sandcastle wall.

The kids started to dig
and the castle walls did fall.

The Incy Wincy Spider
climbed in
the laundry hamper.

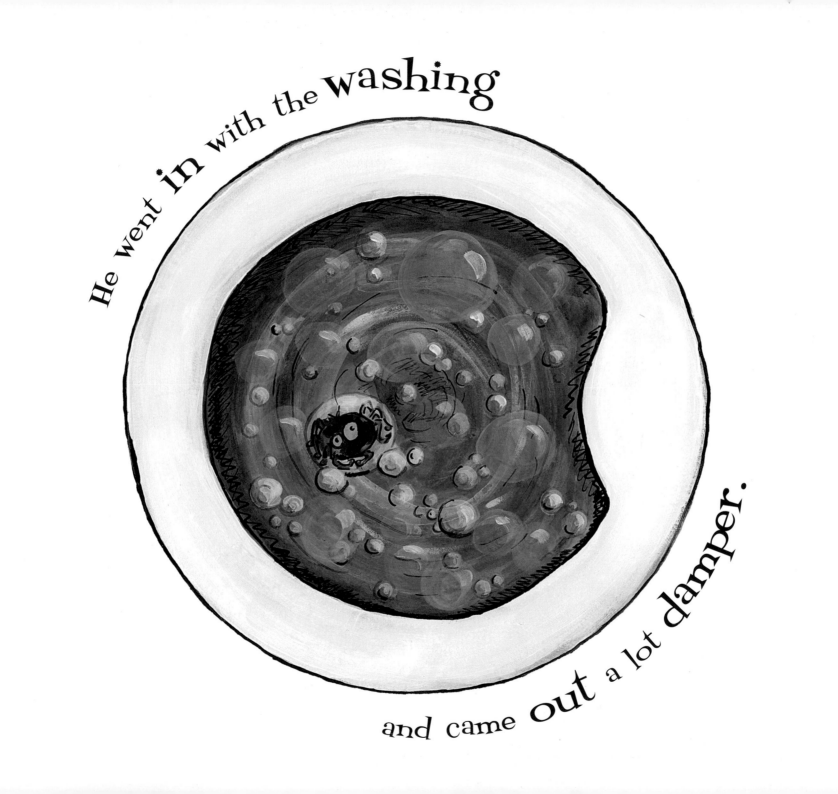

He went **in** with the washing

and came **out** a lot damper.

The Incy Wincy Spider
climbed into a comfy bed.

In jumped the dog and almost squashed Incy dead!

The Incy Wincy Spider
climbed up Grandad's old chair.

Grandma took the **vacuum** and **sucked** Incy **out** of there.

The Incy Wincy Spider
climbed under
the toilet rim.

The Incy Wincy Spider
climbed up out of the wet.

But under the soggy umbrella was as dry as he could get.

Out came the sunshine
and dried up all the rain ...